Learning Soccer

This book was a gift from: _____

```
..........................................
:                                        :
:                                        :
:                                        :
:                                        :
:            Put a photo                 :
:            of yourself                 :
:               here.                    :
:                                        :
:                                        :
:                                        :
:                                        :
..........................................
```

My name: *Jacqueline Michelle Xiang Martineau*

My birthday: *March 12*

My address: *75 Woodman's Chart*

Learning Soccer

Barth/Zempel

Sports Science Consultant:
Dr. Berndt Barth

Meyer & Meyer Sport

The authors would like to thank *Erich Rutemöller*, coach and training supervisor for the *DFB (German Soccer Association)*, for his expert advice.

Original Title: Ich lerne Fußball
Aachen: Meyer & Meyer 2003
Translated by Susanne Evens, Petra Haynes
AAA Translation, St. Louis, Missouri, USA
www.AAATranslation.com

British Library Cataloguing in Publication Data
A catalogue record for this book is available from the British Library

Learning Soccer
Katrin Barth / Ullrich Zempel
Oxford: Meyer & Meyer Sport (UK) Ltd., 2004
ISBN 1-84126-130-0

All rights reserved, especially the right to copy and distribute, including the translation rights. No part of this work may be reproduced – including by photocopy, microfilm or any other means – processed, stored electronically, copied or distributed in any form whatsoever without the written permission of the publisher.

© 2004 by Meyer & Meyer Sport (UK) Ltd.
Aachen, Adelaide, Auckland, Budapest, Graz, Johannesburg, Miami, Olten (CH), Oxford, Singapore, Toronto
Member of the World
Sports Publishers' Association (WSPA)
www.w-s-p-a.org
Printed and bound by: FINIDR, s. r. o., Český Těšín
ISBN 1-84126-130-0
E-Mail: verlag@m-m-sports.com
www.m-m-sports.com

............................TABLE OF CONTENTS

1   **Dear Beginner Soccer Player** 9
    Tips from the authors,
    Billy, the magic soccer mouse introduces himself

2   **How Soccer Began** 15
    Interesting facts about soccer's history,
    soccer in Germany

3   **Hi there, Ulf Kirsten!** 21
    An interview with the successful goal scorer from the
    German Bundesliga, role models, your favorites

4   **No Pain, No Gain** 29
    The right attitude for the sport, about personal goals
    and motivation

5   **Fit and Healthy** 33
    Proper nutrition, healthy life style

6   **Soccer Equipment** 37
    The clothing, the ball, the goal, the field

7   **Keeping Things Straight** 45
    Rules for a fair game, the referee

8   **A Feel for the Ball** 51
    Sure and skillful handling of the ball,
    exercises

9	**A little Something about Soccer Technique** 63	

Shooting goals and passing, the header, frequent mistakes, helpful hints and exercises

10	**Dribbling, Feints, Taking-on and Moving the Ball** 89	

Ball control, feinting the opponent,
taking-on and moving the ball, exercises

11	**Let's Play!** 105	

Lots of ideas for playing in the yard or in a team

12	**Playing for a Soccer Club** 115	

How do I sign up?,
age groups and leagues

13	**Little Soccer Encyclopedia** 121	

Important soccer terminology

14	**Solutions and Answers** 123	

Solutions to puzzles and answers to questions

15	**Let's Talk** 125	

Dear Parents, dear Soccer Coach,
suggestions from the authors on how we can support our little
players and how to use the book effectively

Photo & Illustration Credits 135

Annotation:
The exercises and practical suggestions in this book have been carefully chosen and reviewed by the authors. However, the authors are not liable for accidents or damage of any kind incurred in connection with this book.

LEARNING SOCCER

You will see these pictures of me quite often:

When you see this picture it means I have a tip for you.

Next to this picture you will find exercises you can do at home. Some of them are easy to do by yourself. Parents, grandparents, brothers and sisters, or friends make good practice partners, too.

Pretty tough! The question mark means you can answer questions, or solve puzzles. You'll find the answers at the end of the book on the solutions page.

This means something needs to be filled out or colored in. Use a pencil if you're not really sure, or if you want to update your entries.

.... 1 Dear Beginner Soccer Player

You are probably one of those people who can't walk past a rolling ball, or an empty soda can, or a balled up piece of paper without kicking it. Your foot just gets this itch, and you want to start playing. If a second person comes along you suddenly find yourself fighting over the object. To capture the thing you dig, and dribble, and break free, – just like playing on the field. And if one of the players sees anything remotely resembling a goal, he'll try to aim for it. How great the joy when the shot on goal is successful. Is that how you discovered your love of soccer?

Or may be you watched the World Championships on television, and that gave you the idea to learn to play soccer yourself. In any case, you have chosen the most popular sport in the world.

Learning Soccer

Many boys and girls learn to play soccer in a soccer club. They have regular practices, play on a team, and go to soccer meets. But that doesn't mean you have to be a member of a club to play soccer. A ball, an open space, and a few friends, and you're ready to go.

Whom do you most like to play soccer with? Write down their names, or collect their signatures.

> Melissa Raiven
> Kristen Vanessa
> Ashley   Caitlin
> Sara   Melissa
> Evie   Alex
> Anya
> Rochelle
> Ishanda

What do you like best about playing soccer? Oh, sure, – you like shooting goals! In with the ball, or there is no victory! But to do that you need to have good aim, be able to dribble, do headers, steal the ball, and pass it.

The better you can do those things, the more successful you and your team will be.

Dear Beginner Soccer Player

Listed below are some of the reasons kids like to play soccer.

Which of these apply to you? Check "Yes" or "No"!

	Yes	No
I love sports and running around.	✓	
I like to be with other kids.	✓	
I want to play on a team.	✓	
I can run fast.	✓	
I can handle a ball well.	✓	
I am not afraid to go one-on-one.	✓	
I want to score goals and win.	✓	
My friends can also play soccer.	✓	
I want to be a professional player someday.	✓	

If you answered "Yes" to most of these questions, you have picked the right sport.

In this soccer book we have written down some things worth knowing about your favorite sport. We explain the most important techniques, how you can practice them, and which mistakes to avoid. You will get a number of suggestions for practicing, alone or with your friends. There are also many ideas for games. Of course Mom, Dad, grandparents, brothers and sisters, and anyone who has fun playing is invited to practice with you.

May be you will be a super-successful player in a national team or in a really successful soccer club some day. But even if you just play soccer as

DEAR BEGINNER SOCCER PLAYER

a recreational activity, you will notice that you are getting a lot out of this sport. You learn to play together with others, to become part of a team, and to assert yourself. You learn to fight and to show will power. You won't always be the cheerful winner. But you will learn to deal with defeat, with going one-on-one and losing, with bad passes, or missed penalty kicks. And soon you will notice that by playing soccer regularly you are building stamina, are becoming stronger and more athletic and are keeping your body fit and healthy.

This book is meant to be your companion while learning to play soccer. Sometimes we may view something a little differently from the way your coach or trainer, or another experienced soccer player may explain it to you. That can happen. If that is the case, just ask. Even in soccer there can be different perceptions.

When we talk about trainers, coaches, soccer players, referees, goalies, etc., we are of course also referring to girls and women.

**So have a great time playing soccer and reading this book!
The authors and Billy.**

..................2 How Soccer Began

No one really remembers how this hugely popular sport began a long time ago. But we do know that it began long before there were videos, or photography, or even books. Ancient cave drawings show people playing something similar to soccer.

But that itch in your foot, the desire to kick something around with your feet and to defend it against others, and then to kick it into some kind of goal, – surely our ancestors had that same desire.

Round is the ball

And as is typical for human beings, they worked on developing better balls. At first they bound straw into ball shapes, then they stuffed animal skins, and later they sewed cloth balls. The first leather balls weren't quite perfect either. The leather had no protection, so if the field was wet, the ball soaked up the water and got really heavy.

LEARNING SOCCER

Did you know ...

... that soccer probably began in China? That was about 5000 years ago, when the Emperor's soldiers played ball with their feet.

... that there are 4000-year old drawings inside Egyptian burial caves depicting people playing ball with their thighs and feet?

... that a few hundred years ago Kings forbade soccer playing? Since there were no fixed rules at that time, most games ended in a terrible brawl. That was too dangerous.

 How Soccer Began

... that the first soccer club was founded in England? It was called FC Sheffield.

... that the first international match was played in 1872?
England played against Scotland, and the final score was 0-0.

... that in 1864 the British Football Association determined that the players' pants had to cover their knees?

... that the first international match between Germany and England was played in Berlin in 1899? It ended in a 2-13 loss for Germany.

... that England is considered the mother country of soccer?

How many old leather soccer balls are hidden on these two pages?
Before you start counting look away and make a guess!

Enter the number you guessed here: 5

Enter the actual number here: 5

# Learning Soccer

Rules are necessary

If there are no rules on where the field begins and where it ends, how big the goal should be, how many players are on a team, or what is allowed and what isn't, soon there would be total chaos. Soccer games often turned into brawls because too many players were kicking at the ball, or players captured the ball by fighting over it and there was no referee to keep order. Today there are internationally adopted regulations for soccer games.

Here you see two pictures of Billy's great-great-grandfather. Find the 10 differences!

Soccer is a team sport

In soccer there are always two teams competing against each other, to score goals, and to win. Teams were formed, clubs established, and championships were held.

Soccer organizations

Every country has a soccer association for all soccer players.

In Germany it is the Deutscher Fußball-Bund (DFB).

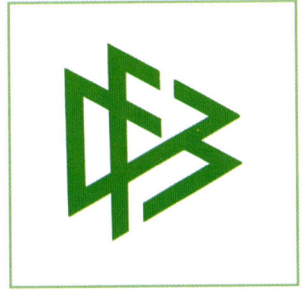

What is it called in your country? Paste or draw the logo here.

The league

The teams play in different divisions. In Germany the major league is called the *Bundesliga*. What do you call the highest level of play in your country? ....

On the next page write down which teams are playing at the highest level this season, and check off the current champions. You will need to use a pencil if you are going to update the list every year.

Also, start a list of champions!

The best teams of 20___

The champions

Year	Champions

..........3 HI THERE, ULF KIRSTEN!

Ulf Kirsten
Born 12.04.1965
Profession: Soccer player for Bayer 04 Leverkusen, Germany (until 2003).

Hi Ulf! What do you love about soccer?

Soccer to me is the struggle for victory and success between two teams in front of an enthusiastic crowd of spectators. It is scoring goals and competing against each other to see who is better. Soccer is playing with a team where the individual can be outstanding, but without the team and the other team mates he won't win. It is a game with clearly defined rules everyone knows. In fact, all you really need is a field, two goals, and a ball, and you're ready to go!

Learning Soccer

What must a good soccer player be able to do?

Soccer makes demands on the entire athlete. He must be quick, must have good control of the ball and not the other way around, with the ball controlling you. The player needs lots of stamina to be able to run and fight for the whole playing time. Kicking the ball requires strong legs, heading the ball requires physical control and flexibility. Soccer is also a single combat sport where I am always fighting for possession of the ball. When I have the ball it must be kept by my team for as long as possible. That is why, when there is a turnover, I must be determined to fight for the ball, even if it hurts sometimes and I have to play against a strong opponent.

What is so special about soccer?

Soccer is also a tactical game. I have to try to hide my intentions from my opponent. I trick him with some subtle movements, or I get free in such a way that it will create gaps in his defense, and one of my team-mates gets a clear shot on the goal.

In soccer you are not a single combatant but are part of a team. Whoever is in the best spot gets the pass and shoots the goal. It is the success of all those who set it up. That is called team spirit.

When did you start to play soccer, and what happened after that?

I have always liked soccer. As a child I started to play for Chemie Riesa in 1972. Later I played for Stahl Riesa and Dynamo Dresden.

I have been playing for Bayer 04 Leverkusen since 1990. You might have even seen me on the national team. In 12 years I have been in 347 Bundesliga games, have shot 181 goals, and have been the number one scorer several times.

Hi there, Ulf Kirsten!

Do you have a tip for beginner players?

First of all you have to really enjoy playing soccer. But you have to realize that without diligence, practice, and discipline you will not be successful. If you want to play soccer join a good club. Soon you'll play on a team and make good friends. Be reliable and be on time for practices and games. To improve your technique and stamina go to training regularly and practice lots at home. But with all the practicing with the ball don't forget school, your friends and your family. Maybe you have some other hobbies that take up some of your time. Soccer isn't everything, especially when you are still so young.

For me soccer is my profession and I can't think of a better one. Do you want to become a professional, too? Then start today and learn all about soccer! This book will surely help you with it.

Thank you for the interview and good luck for the future.

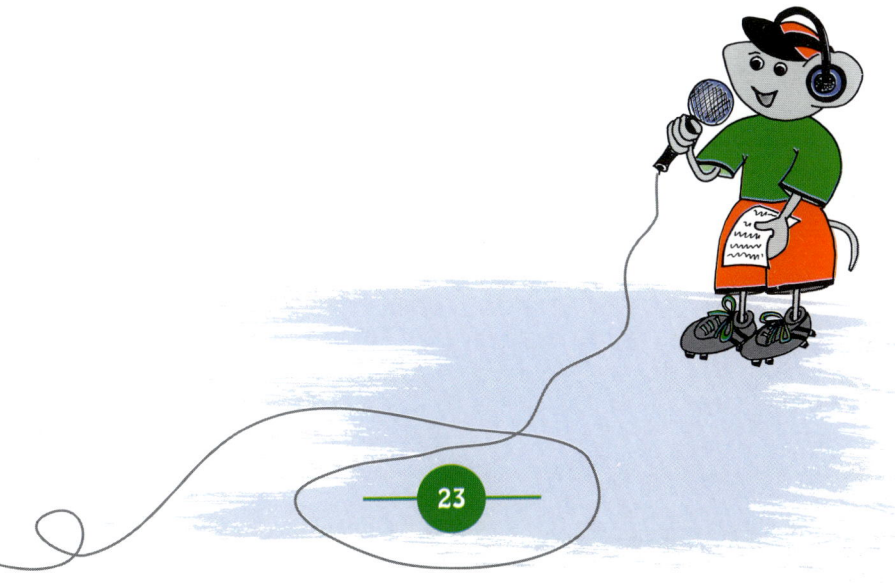

Fan pages

Most kids start playing soccer because they have seen it played on television. They are inspired by the world famous soccer stars and hold them as idols.

Here you can record all of the facts about your idols and your favorite teams. If there isn't enough space just add some pages.

Here is a place for autographs.

My favorite player:

Photo

Name: ....

Team: ....

Position: ....

Special characteristics: ....

....

What I would like to ask him:

....

....

My favorite national team:

....

Team colors: ....

Logo

The best players: ....

....

The biggest wins: ....

....

My favorite international team:

....

Team colors: ....

Logo

The best players: ....

....

The biggest wins: ....

....

HI THERE, ULF KIRSTEN!

Here's a place for photos.

LEARNING SOCCER

........................4 No Pain, No Gain

Surely you have dreamed about what it would be like to be the very best. Everyone cheers for you, admires you, and gazes at you in wonder. All of the most successful clubs want you on their team. The fans are crowding you, asking for autographs. As highest scorer and super forward you are being congratulated by your team-mates, your trainers, your fans, your friends and your parents…!

But stop right there! Just lying in the grass day dreaming isn't enough. If you want to become a good soccer player, and may be even be better than the rest, you need to practice diligently and often. That's not always easy to do and may not be fun right away.

It takes hard work to be successful!

Goals

Answer the following questions:

 What is my goal?

 With what can I reach my goal?

 How can I reach my goal?

What is my goal? Why do I practice so much?

Just kicking the ball around is fun. But soon you want to be able to sprint faster, handle the ball more skillfully, and score more often. Your friends should choose you for their team because you play so well and are always trying to score. Maybe you are ready to play in a good club team or advance in the league as starter. What would it be like to be discovered by a coach for the national soccer league and play professionally in a top team? Of course you are still too small and too young for that now. But you should already have some bigger goals. You have to know what you want. If you don't have a goal, soon the practicing won't be fun anymore. So you keep on setting higher goals for yourself. That's what the successful professional players did too.

List your goals here!

_____

_____

With what can I reach my goal?

Of course you are going to ask what you can do to improve your performance. Definitely play lots and lots of soccer. In addition you will need to do the necessary exercises for technique, running, stamina, and strength, which the soccer coach will do with you. There will likely be some things you won't enjoy doing a whole lot. Some things may seem boring or too strenuous. But always keep in mind that these exercises will help you reach your goal.

If you want to be able to last through an entire game until the final whistle, you need lots of stamina. That's what the running exercises are for. You need to be agile and limber if you want to keep the opponent from taking the ball away from you. For that you'll do gymnastics and stretching exercises. And only those who practice shooting on goal over and over again will actually score in the heat of the moment during a game. If you know all of these things you will train more diligently and do additional exercises at home. Soon you will see your progress and you will see yourself getting better and better.

How can I reach my goal?

How are things going, now that you see yourself getting better through lots of practice? As long as the exercises are easy and relaxed, your muscles will only do what they can already do anyway. Only when something is strenuous and the movement isn't so easy anymore are your muscles being strengthened. So you really need to try hard and push yourself to make progress. If you haven't been to soccer practice in a while you'll notice that you have regressed a little and get winded much faster. Now you have to make up for lost time! So, the more diligently and the more often you practice the better you will be.

# Learning Soccer

Who kicked the ball into the goal?

Sextuplets? Look again! Only two of the mice are identical.

............................5 FIT AND HEALTHY

Most people who are involved in a sport want to have fun and be successful. But another important goal is keeping your body fit and healthy.

Learning to eat right

Athletes use up more energy than couch potatoes. That's why food always tastes best after practice; you are hungry and thirsty and need to replenish your energy supply.

After practice Billy is really hungry. He would like to eat and drink everything all at once.

What would you suggest he do? Cross out the things you think are not very healthy!

Learning Soccer

Almost all kids love candy bars, chips, fries, and pizza. Of course that's not exactly athlete's food, especially if you eat these things often and in large quantities. These foods contain too much fat.

A better meal for an athlete would be whole-wheat bread with cheese, fruit and yoghurt. There are lots of foods that are healthy and taste good. Try to have a varied diet and eat in moderation.

If you sweat you need to drink regularly

When you sweat you lose a lot of fluids which you need to replenish by drinking sufficiently. Water, juice mixes (juice mixed with water), or tea (even sweetened with honey) are best for quenching your thirst. Pure juices or sodas are not suitable as liquid replacements. They contain too much sugar.

When you are thirsty and getting a drink, make sure you don't drink too hastily.

Oh boy! My stomach is so full! And I was just really thirsty.

It is better to take small sips more frequently. Be careful not to overfill your stomach, because you will have a hard time moving around.

Don't take glass bottles on the soccer field! They can break easily and another player may cut himself if he falls.

Hello, Doc!

You'll cheerfully say: "Hello, Doc!" to your doctor because as an athlete you usually feel totally fit. But even if you are not sick you need to visit your doctor at least once a year for a check up. Tell the doctor that you play soccer. He or she will examine you and tell you that you can play without any concerns.

Have your vaccination record updated and get some nutritional tips.

A successful day begins with a good start in the morning!

Some tips from Billy:

 Go to bed on time and get plenty of sleep!

 Look forward to the new day.

 Stretch after getting up. How about some morning gymnastics? You'll find some exercises on the next page.

 After cleaning up, a cold shower is just the thing. It's refreshing and toughens you up.

 Whole-wheat bread, cereal, milk, yoghurt, and fruit are part of a good and healthy breakfast.

 Don't forget to brush your teeth after you eat!

LEARNING SOCCER

On this page there are some exercises you can do in the morning.

Lie down flat on your back and lift up your pelvis.

Stand up on your toes and reach up with your arms, like you are trying to pick an apple off a tree.

Then suddenly collapse and make yourself really small.

Twist your hips side to side.

Bend to the right side.

Bend to the left side.

6 Soccer Equipment

Even a beginner soccer player wants to look like the real thing. What does it take? Of course you need a jersey with the colors of your favorite team and with your number and name on the back. Then you also need the matching shorts and socks. Proper soccer boots with studs are also important. Shin guards will keep you from getting bruised shins.

As a goalie you will also need the "hold-any-ball gloves"!

All that looks great but in the beginning it's not necessary. You can play soccer in any clothes. They must be comfortable and not interfere with your running. Since you'll sometimes fall down in the fight for the ball, you probably shouldn't wear your best clothes. If you play in a league, the teams will wear uniforms.

 Learning Soccer

Soccer boots

When you play soccer you have to run fast, dribble the ball, stop, and kick the ball. Can you do that with your shoes? Would your shoes hold up? Then they are just right. In fact the thinner tennis shoes are better for learning to get a feel for the ball and for handling the ball skillfully. If you play in a league and on a team you should soon get real soccer boots. What makes them special are the studs under the soles. They give you better traction on the grass. Later you will need replaceable studs. Get some advice at the shoe store because soccer boots should fit well and feel good on your feet.

Shin guards for safety

When you are fighting hard for the ball you do get some bruises. But you should wear shin guards to avoid more severe injuries or even fractures. Shin guards are mandatory in competitions, not only for the players but also for the goalie.

Is Christmas or your birthday coming up?

Surely your parents, grandparents, aunts and uncles ask you what you want. How about a pair of soccer boots, shin guards, or goalie gloves?

Everything packed?

Imagine you have just arrived at a game and you notice in the locker room that you forgot your boots! Your super-fast, well broken in boots are at home, far, far away! You can't borrow any because they won't fit. If you are not able to play it isn't just disappointing for you, but for the whole team.

Of course your mom can help with packing your bag, but it is each player's responsibility to have complete and proper equipment.

LEARNING SOCCER

Use a check list like the one on the next page. Everything in your bag gets checked off. Use a pencil so you can always erase the check marks. Write down anything else you shouldn't forget on the blank lines.

Check list

Jersey ☐

Shorts ☐

Socks ☐

Shin guards ☐

Boots ☐

Soap/Shampoo ☐

_____ ☐

_____ ☐

_____ ☐

_____ ☐

SOCCER EQUIPMENT

The soccer ball

Maybe you've played soccer with an empty soda can before. But it's really only fun with a ball. But it doesn't have to be an expensive leather ball. In the beginning it's easier to play and practice with a light rubber ball. Or how about a tennis ball?

In competitions the size and weight of the ball are regulated and the referee inspects the ball before the game begins. It is also important that the ball has enough air in it.

A tip for buying a ball:

Children   age 6 to age 7 – size 3
  age 8 to age 10 – size 4 (light)
  from age 11/12 – size 5 (light)

What is that?

Which one is the missing piece?

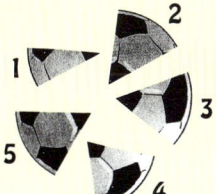

The soccer goal

Normally you need two goals when you are playing soccer, because for a soccer player, kicking the ball into the goal is the best. But you can start out playing with only one goal. However, a goal you must have! But where do you get a goal when you are playing in the school yard or on the street?

Picnic benches, a couple of trees, or rocks make good goals. Just put down some objects to mark the goalposts, and you're ready to play!

When you set up your goal make sure the ball can't roll too far after it gets kicked into goal. A wall or a hedge behind the goal makes the ball rebound to you. No player enjoys having to constantly go to get the ball.

SOCCER EQUIPMENT

On a real soccer field there will be goals with netting. The size of the goals is laid down in the regulations. For children up to age 12, the goals are a little smaller.

The playing field

Soccer can be played anywhere. Some communities have public soccer fields or play areas, or you can play in your schoolyard or on a quiet neighborhood street. Ask if you're not sure whether it's alright to play somewhere!

Real competitions are played on real soccer fields. But because the young soccer players don't have the same endurance as the older players, there are special fields for them.

The younger ones play across one half of a large field.

 *Learning Soccer*

Some tips from Billy:

- ⚽ Try not to disturb anyone!

- ⚽ Be careful not to break any windows, or to damage cars or flower beds!

- ⚽ Watch out for small children or people walking by!

- ⚽ Be careful not to dirty new or freshly painted surfaces!

- ⚽ Watch out for traffic!

> Hey! That was our goalpost!

7 Keeping Things Straight

Almost everything in our lives has some kind of order. It would be pretty chaotic if everyone just did as they pleased. There are rules within a family, as well as in the kindergarten and at school. There are traffic laws, and every card game has its own rules.

It is the same with sports. Every sport has rules about how it is played, how a competition proceeds, and when a team loses or wins. The rules also define what is permitted and what isn't.

Soccer has a whole book full of rules. It's a good thing, too! Do you remember how it used to be when there were no real soccer rules? Often the game turned into a big brawl.

But we are not going to write about all of the soccer rules. That's much too difficult and at this point not that important to you. When you play with friends you make your own rules, and on the team your coach will explain everything to you. If you are really interested you can read all of the soccer rules in the Soccer Federation rule book.

LEARNING SOCCER

A game with friends

Even if you are just playing with your friends at school or in the yard, you still need to discuss certain things. Before the game begins you make up your own rules.

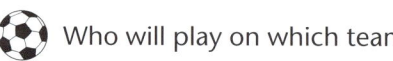 Who will play on which team?

 Where will the goals be?

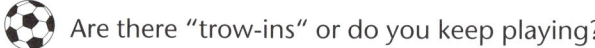 Are there "trow-ins" or do you keep playing?

 Are there corners?

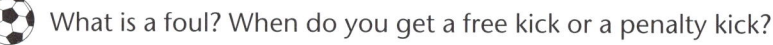 What is a foul? When do you get a free kick or a penalty kick?

Sometimes you'll notice while you're playing that something needs to be clarified. Discuss it! To avoid conflict you can choose one of the players as referee.

If no coach, trainer or teacher is present the players determine their own rules. Everyone has a say! The rules are not made by the biggest person or by the person who owns the ball.

Foul play is unfair

No one likes playing soccer alone. Or do you think it's fun to dribble by yourself, or to keep shooting the ball at a goal that doesn't have a goalie in it?

The other players aren't your enemies but your opponents. You need them to play, so treat them fairly!

You can't play soccer without the other players.

Treat your opponent fairly and try not to hurt him or her.

Apologize if you accidentally commit a foul.

Playing one-on-one fairly

The most exiting thing in soccer is the one-on-one play. You want to receive the ball first, steal it away, dribble it around the opponent, and dummy round him. You try to take the ball away from the opposing team and keep it with your team until it scores. There are many opportunities to do this and you shouldn't be afraid or nervous. But anything you do during a one-on-one play should not hurt the opponent.

Here you can see illustrations of soccer players fighting hard for the ball. Use a red pencil to circle the pictures that show forbidden actions such as a foul or dangerous play!

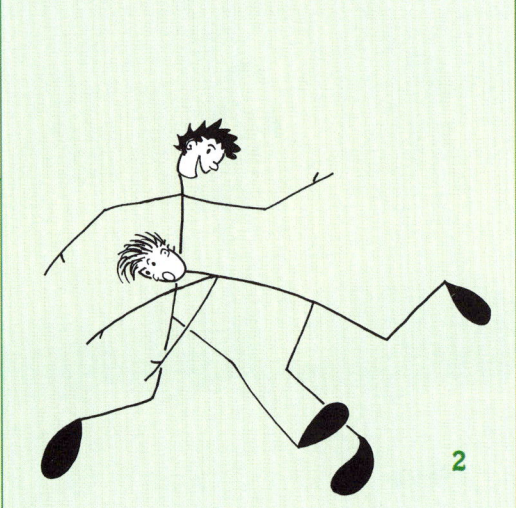

KEEPING THINGS STRAIGHT

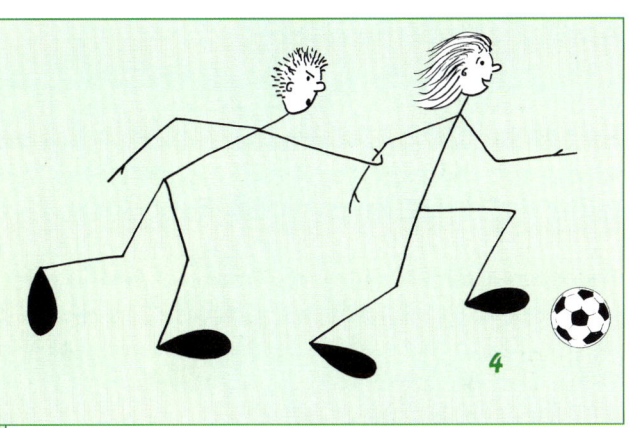

A word about the referee

In the old days, the referee was also called the man in black. That's because he was always dressed in black. Nowadays the refs also wear jerseys and shorts in red, green or other colors. What's important is that the ref can be distinguished from the players and is easily recognizable.

The referee directs the game, makes sure the rules are obeyed and also issues penalties. He has to run pretty fast to always stay level with the ball. He also has to make quick decisions on goals, throw-ins, fouls, or penalty kicks. That's pretty difficult because he doesn't have instant replay to help him like we do on television.

You don't need a referee when you play with your friends. You can work out the rules amongst yourselves. But maybe you would like to be a referee sometime. Try it! You'll see how difficult it is, and that not everyone is always happy with your decisions.

As referee what call do you have to make here?

Do you know what these referee hand signals mean?

1 _____ 2 _____ 3 _____

........................8 A Feel for the Ball

What exactly is a feel for the ball?

Is it the ball's excitement when it lands in the goal?

Or is it the pain the ball feels when it is kicked hard?

> Oh, my dear ball! I love you so much! I am sorry for always kicking you so hard!

Or is it the feelings the soccer player has for his ball?

LEARNING SOCCER

Ball control

Dribbling and feinting

Taking-on and dribbling the ball

What a soccer player needs to be able to do:

Headers

Stealing the ball

Shooting at goal and passing

A Feel for the Ball

Having a *feel for the ball* means how well a player is able to feel the ball. With his foot he feels the ball's weight, its size, and the material it is made of. He feels how the ball bounces, rolls, and flies. A good soccer player has to have that feel.

Many feet and only one ball. Whoever handles the ball best on the field will win.

For that you must:

- *Take on the ball with your foot, head, or body.*
- *Dribble and move the ball without your opponent taking it away from you.*
- *Pass the ball confidently and accurately.*
- *Aim well and score.*

In a game you need to control the ball. You decide with your foot what to do with the ball. Should it stay with you, or how far and where will it fly to. You are the boss and will make the ball do your bidding, and not the other way around!

It would be easier to use your hands, but only the goalie is allowed to do so. That's why it is important that you train your feet really well. A top player can feel as well with his feet as he can with his hands.

Only with lots and lots of practice can you get this feel for the ball. Even the best players continue to do ball exercises. It would be best if you took a little time to practice every day. You'll find exercises on the next few pages. Have fun!

You can even practice while watching television!

Exercises to feel the ball

For these exercises also refer to Chapter 9 on kicking technique. That's where the techniques for the different types of kicks are explained.

How can you practice?
While standing up, sitting down on the floor or sitting in a chair. Put on your soccer boots or wear regular shoes. But you feel the ball best when barefoot.

Where can you practice?
You don't need much space for the exercises. You can practice outside, in the yard or even inside, if it doesn't disturb anyone.

What can you practice with?
The soccer ball is your tool. If there is no real soccer ball available, other balls will do just fine. Use large, small, soft, and hard balls.

How quickly do you have to practice?
Of course a player should be very quick with the ball. But that doesn't happen right away. First you do the exercises slowly and then you try to do them a little quicker each time. Eventually you need to be quick and accurate!

A soccer player has to work both legs equally hard. In a game you can't always choose with which foot you kick the ball. Accepting and kicking the ball has to be done with the left and the right foot. Be careful to train evenly if you notice that you have a strong and a weak foot.

So keep switching from one foot to the other!

1 Rolling the ball

One foot is placed on top of the ball. Now roll the ball forward and backward, to the right and to the left, and in a circle. Keep your foot firmly on the ball. Don't lose it!

2 Sliding the foot over the ball

In this exercise the foot slides from one side of the ball to the other side while maintaining constant contact with the ball. Once your foot reaches the other side you start moving it back again. It is easier when the supporting leg hops along a little.

You can practice with one leg standing up or sitting down.

Now slide both feet over the ball! (Can you do it standing up?)

3 Rolling the ball

Roll the ball with the bottom of your foot. Hop along with your supporting leg. Move forwards and backwards, with your right foot and your left.

4 Forward – stop – backwards – stop

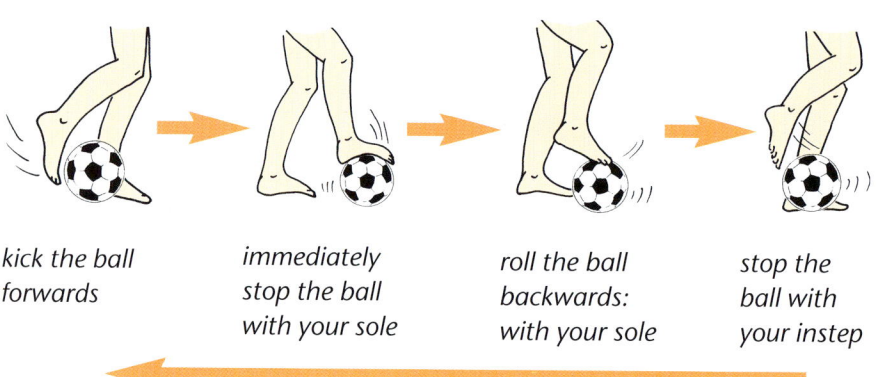

| kick the ball forwards | immediately stop the ball with your sole | roll the ball backwards: with your sole | stop the ball with your instep |

... And now start over again!

You'll have to kick gently so the ball doesn't roll too far!

A Feel for the Ball

Keep a record of how many times a week you practice! Write down the week on the upper line, and then make a tally mark underneath for each time you practice.

Week	1.	2.						
Number	⃗℩℩℩⃗/							

5 Slalom

Set up a slalom course and guide the ball through it with your foot. Keep the ball close to your foot so you don't lose it.

There are several ways you and your friends, or even just you alone can have a contest.

 How many times can you complete the course in both directions without losing the ball? (Or, allow one mistake!)

 If you have a stopwatch you can determine the fastest competitor.

6 Shooting on target

Pick a starting point and then pick a target a short distance away. You can even draw a kind of target on the ground. The target shouldn't be too far away since we are working on getting a feel for the ball, and not long distance shots.

 Who will get closest to the target?

 Who scores the most points?

Juggling the ball

Who amongst us hasn't admired those acrobats who can keep a ball in the air for the longest time using many points of contact? The ball makes contact alternately with foot, thigh or head. But those aren't just much admired tricks.

Every soccer player should be a ball acrobat.

Therefore try the following juggling exercises. Since it isn't all that easy, try these preliminary exercises first.

 Drop the ball and then play it back up so you can catch it before it hits the ground. You will need to catch the ball fully on your instep and bring it back up with some sensitivity.

LEARNING SOCCER

- Try the same exercise using your thigh. Drop the ball and then play it back up with the thigh of the bent leg.

- For juggling with your head gently toss the ball in the air. Butt the ball with your head and then catch it with your hands.

A Feel for the Ball

 Juggle first to the right and then to the left.

 Keep switching legs.

 Alternate between foot, thigh, and leg.

 Juggle only with your head.

If at first you are having trouble it's OK for the ball to bounce occasionally before you play it with your foot.

 *Count how many times you can make contact with the ball without interruption. Use a pencil to record your personal record in the box below the illustration. Since you will hopefully continue to improve, you can erase the old number and record your latest record.*

A good player can do at least 50 repetitions!

 Learning Soccer

Picking up the ball

In order to juggle you first need to get the ball on your foot, knee, or head. Most likely you will use your hands at first. But then try to pick up the ball with your foot.

Roll the ball backwards with your sole ➡ *slide your foot under the ball* ➡ *and up onto your instep*

It is frustrating when the ball keeps falling off and rolling away during those first exercises. Besides, you end up spending more time chasing the ball than actually practicing.

Billy has a good idea!
- *Tie the ball to a long piece of string, or put it in a net with a long tie. Hold the end of the string in your hand or tie it to something.*
- *Use a shorter length of string for the foot shot and a longer one for the header.*

9 A LITTLE SOMETHING ABOUT SOCCER TECHNIQUE

GOAL!!!

What could be better in soccer than scoring a goal? Sometimes it's like a gun shot, other times a lob over the goalie, a bicycle kick or a header. These kinds of goals always excite us.

Scoring goals like these is the result of diligent practice and training. You have to try to shoot at goal over and over again from all positions. It is important that you know the shooting technique, the foot position and body movement. You learn to estimate distances by doing different exercises, and you try to figure out how much power you need to put into a shot.

Learning Soccer

Shooting at goal and passing are what's most important for the beginner player. That's why this book will focus mostly on those areas.

On the following pages, we will explain most of the kicks you would use to shoot at goal or to pass to a team-mate. We will describe the execution, and the mistakes you might be making. You will get tips for practicing with your team or at home.

When you're playing, you will figure out yourself which kick or pass you should use in which situation. Maybe you can even learn by watching experienced players or by watching soccer on television.

A LITTLE SOMETHING ABOUT SOCCER TECHNIQUE

The direction of the ball

The direction in which the ball travels depends on where the ball was struck. The illustration shows the contact points and the direction of travel. Get a ball and try it out!

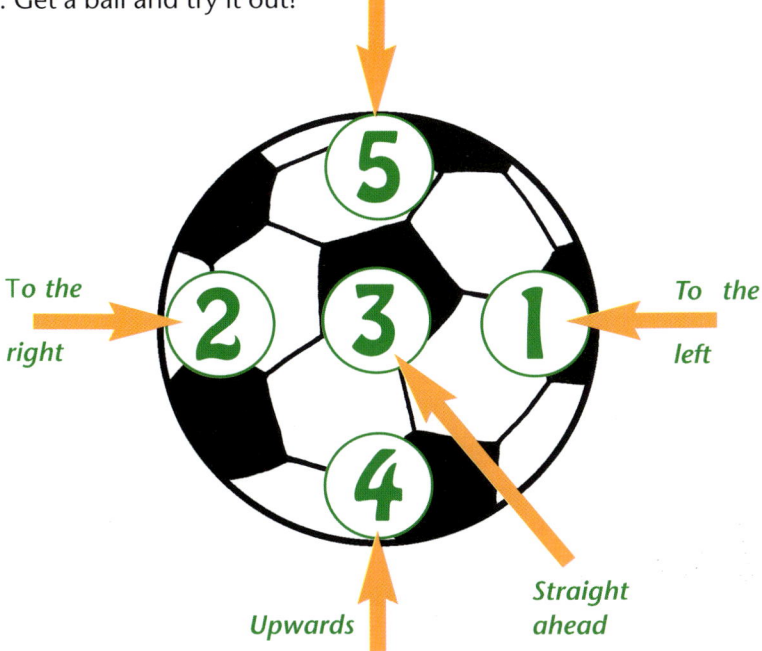

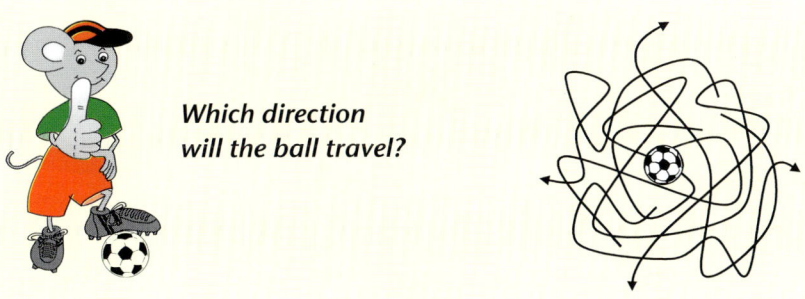

Which direction will the ball travel?

The contact areas on the boot

Another critical factor is which part of the foot makes contact with the ball. That is important for the direction the ball will travel, the ferocity of the shot, and the spin on the ball. But you can't pick a favorite side. It is the particular situation in the game that's decisive. Every soccer player has to learn to use all sides.

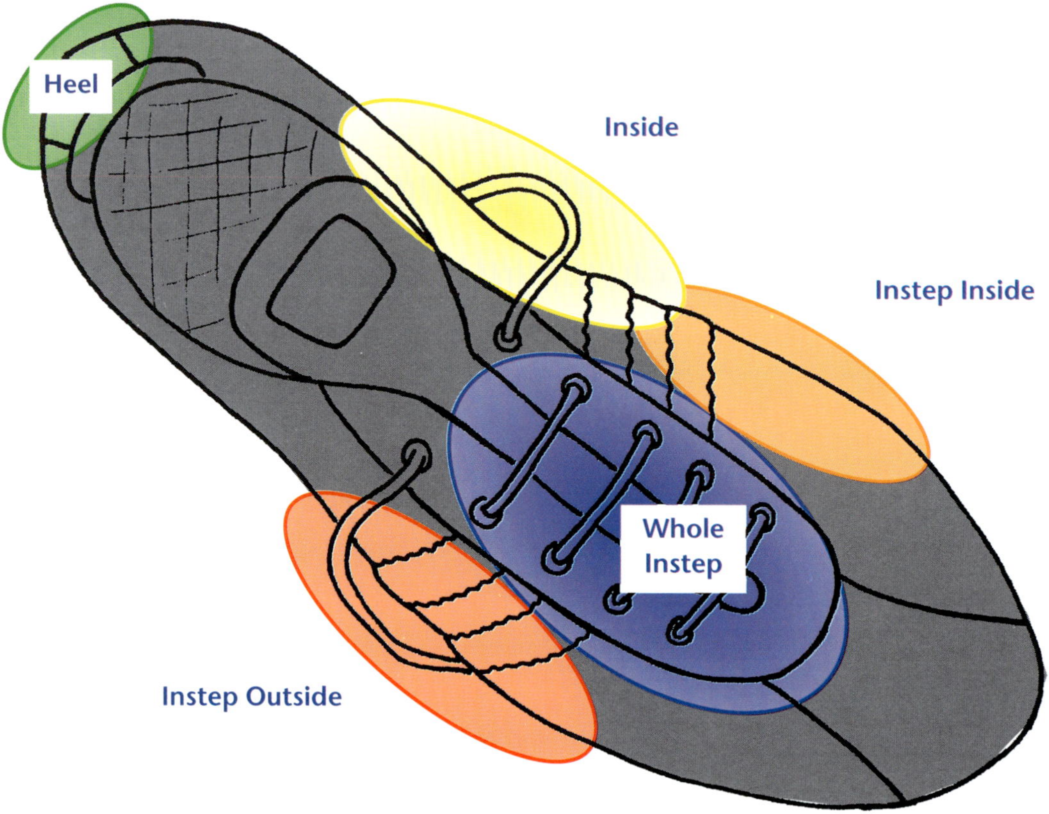

Heel

Inside

Instep Inside

Whole Instep

Instep Outside

The kicks are named according to the side of the foot you use to make the kick. You will see this on the following pages.

A little Something about Soccer Technique

The kick with the inside of the foot (inside kick)

The inside kick is the most commonly used and most accurate kick. The inside of the foot gives you a good feel for the ball and enables you to make a more accurate pass. That is important for short passes to team mates or for penalty kicks. The inside kick isn't well suited for hard long balls.

This is how it's done:

- The foot of the supporting leg is placed sideways – about a foot's width – next to the ball.
- The toe of the supporting leg points in the direction of the kick.
- The knee of the kicking leg is slightly bent.
- The feet are at a right angle to each other.
- The kicking leg is swung in the direction of play.
- Hit the ball right in the middle.
- Slightly bend your torso over the ball.

LEARNING SOCCER

The player in these illustrations is trying to kick the ball with an inside kick. He probably won't be very successful. What is he doing wrong?

Do you have the same problem? Mark here what you need to work on. But use a pencil so you can hopefully erase the mark again soon!

1

2

3

A LITTLE SOMETHING ABOUT SOCCER TECHNIQUE

Make sure you warm up a bit before you start the kicking exercises. If your muscles are cold you can pull a muscle while kicking. That's painful and very annoying.

Some light jogging exercises or some easy jumps are good for warming up. Stretch a little and you're ready to go!

This is how you can practice:

 Start with some exercises without the ball.

 Practice the kick with the inside of the foot on a pre-drawn line (i.e. the boundary line of the playing field or a chalk line). The ball should roll exactly along the line.

 First practice from a standing position without a running start. The supporting leg is already positioned next to the ball and you just give the ball a quick tap.

 Aim for small goals from a short distance.
Have a contest:
  • 10 shots from the line into a small 1-meter goal.
  • Keep the score.

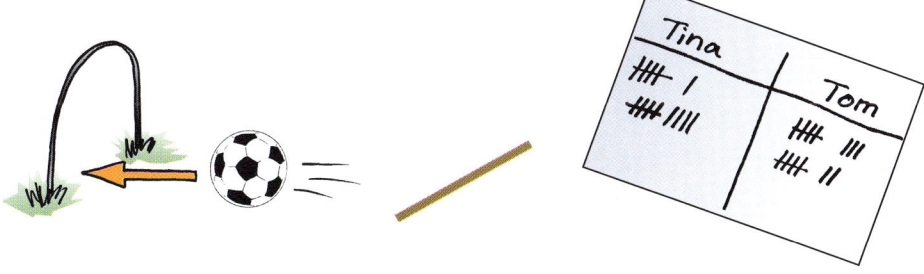

Kicking with the instep

The areas of contact for instep kicks are marked on the soccer shoe illustration. You can see that there are three types of instep kicks:

- Inner instep
- Outer instep
- Full instep

The inner instep kick

With the inner instep you are able to play the ball very far and very high. That is why the inner instep kick is almost always used for free kicks, corner kicks, passing, or goal kicks. It is also suitable for flank shots and long passes. It also allows you to lob the ball high over the opponent.

The outer instep kick

The outer instep kick lets you do accurate, long passes. You also use it to pass to free yourself, for corner kicks, free kicks, or shots at goal. You use it to dribble around your opponent. The ball has a curved trajectory and a spin. This is called 'putting side' on a ball.

The full-instep kick (instep drive)

You kick hardest by using your full instep. That's why it is most often used for shots at goal, long passes, or for clearance by the defense. It is also suitable for long goal kicks or free kicks.

This is how instep kicks are done:

- The foot of the supporting leg stands sideways – about a foot's breadth – next to the ball.
- The toe of the supporting leg points in the direction of the kick.
- The playing leg swings from the hip, then from the knee, and then very quick and hard forward to the ball.
- The ankle of the playing leg is rigid.
- You swing the playing leg through in the direction of play.
- With an instep kick you hit the ball fully with your instep (on your laces), the inside or outside of your instep.
- After the shot the torso is bent over the ball and the supporting leg.

A Little Something about Soccer Technique

Carefully look at the illustrations! What is wrong with their instep drive?

Do you have the same problem? Mark here what you need to work on. But use a pencil so you can hopefully erase the mark again soon!

leaning back too much when kicking

1

using her toe wich is a part of your foot you can hurt when kicking.

2

legs are to far apart. If they were closer he could have more power into his kick.

3

 Learning Soccer

This is how you can practice:

 Just practice without the ball first.

 Use a pre-drawn line for your running start (i.e. playing field boundary or a chalk line).

 From a moderate distance play against a wall with your inner instep. Try to kick the ball as soon as it comes back to you. How many times can you do it without making a mistake?

 Draw a target on a wall and try to hit it with the ball.

 Take turns kicking the ball to each other with the inner instep.

How long can you kick it back and forth without making a mistake? It's more difficult if you move around while you play.

A Little Something about Soccer Technique

 Find a fence or a barricade or hang a tire from a rope. Now kick the ball back and forth. This is where accuracy counts.

 Set up a small goal. Set a distance of approximately 10 strides. Mark a starting point and try to score a goal using the outside instep.

- *How many goals can you score with 10 attempts?*
- *Write down your score.*
- *Can you improve over the next few days?*
- *Do this contest with your friends.*
- *Who gets the highest score?*

 Learning Soccer

 Find a target and try to hit it. It can be a tree, a pail, or some stacked up cans.

How many times do you score with 20 attempts?

 Do you have plenty of space? No pedestrians, windows or cars close by? Then let's see how far your instep drive (full instep) will go!

It's great if your friend can stop the ball. Then he'll be able to kick it right back.

Always alternate your legs and feet! You don't want to train one-sided.

A LITTLE SOMETHING ABOUT SOCCER TECHNIQUE

The header

In soccer the header is something special. When a high ball comes in, a player can play it with his head. This could be a header at the goal, a pass to a team mate or defensive play.

This is how a header is done:

- The ball is butted with the forehead.
- The neck is rigid.
- The eyes stay open or you won't see the ball.
- Jump at the right moment.
- The torso is taut like a bow.
- The torso shoots forward and the powerful butt is made with the whole body.

What's special about the header

- You can do a header from a standing position, from a jump or from a dive.
- Your body movement determines the direction the ball will travel.
- A header can be just as powerful as a shot at goal, if the pass is done with accuracy and power.

Some people say that headers are only for tall players, and that smaller players don't have a chance. But that's not necessarily true.

It is also the player who jumps the highest or who jumps at the right moment that gets the ball. Anyone who is quick and can jump high has an advantage in the fight for the ball.

A LITTLE SOMETHING ABOUT SOCCER TECHNIQUE

Look closely at these illustrations. What are these players doing wrong with their headers?

 Learning Soccer

This is how you can practice:

- First complete the movement without the ball.
- Use a soft ball in the beginning.
- At first try doing the header from a standing position.
- Toss the ball in the air yourself.
- Let someone else throw the ball to you at head height.

Don't be afraid of the header! Your forehead is tough enough and the head is sufficiently protected by your skull bones. Nothing should happen if the header is executed properly.

By the way: If you blow your math's test it's not because you've been practicing headers!

Practice tips for doing the header

 With a friend try to play the ball back and forth with your heads.

 If you are alone head the ball against a wall.

 The header-goal game is a lot of fun. Set up two goals (14 feet wide) about 18 feet apart, and try to score against your opponent by doing headers. Throw the ball to each other straight up and head the ball as hard as you can from a standing position into the opposite goal.

 To practice headers from a jump, throw the ball yourself and then head it. It's best to head it against a wall so you don't have to keep running after it.

 Have a partner throw the ball to you. This can be done from the front, or from the front and side.

 Long distance header contest
Who can head the ball the farthest after tossing it into the air? Wherever the ball lands marks the distance.
(A tip: throw very high and keep your body taut!)

With lots of practice you will gradually get a feel for when to jump and how much power to use.

Are you tired of chasing after the ball? Remember the ball in the net or the ball on the string in Chapter 8.

LEARNING SOCCER

Here is something for you to color. Have fun!

The goalie

Scoring goals is fun! And it's not all that easy. But it's only really fun when you have to get past a goalie. How can you sell him a dummy and send him to the wrong corner? Or is your shot such a rocket that the goalie doesn't stand a chance?

Whether you are shooting at a goal made up from two school satchels, or in a game with two teams, it is an exciting task to be the last man. The one everyone else relies on and the one who keeps his goal safe. You are not playing positions yet, so take turns acting as goalie.

A goalie must:

- *be able to catch well.*
- *assess the situation accurately.*
- *always be vigilant.*
- *be brave.*

But two big, sturdy gloves aren't enough to make you a good goalie. Here are a few tips!

LEARNING SOCCER

Holding the ball

Once you have caught the ball hold on to it tightly. Hold it to your chest with both arms. Spread your fingers when you catch to increase your catching surface. Bend your body toward the ball so a hard ball doesn't knock you down.

If the ball is low, catch it kneeling down. Be careful to keep your legs closed while you are kneeling so the ball doesn't roll between your legs.

Catch a medium-high ball with your legs slightly bent. The arms and legs move like the shovel of an excavator. Make yourself nice and round.

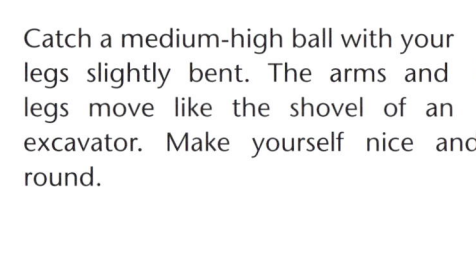

For high balls you really have to jump. Spread your thumbs when you catch, so the ball is secure and won't slip through your hands. Once you've caught the ball hold it tightly to your chest.

A LITTLE SOMETHING ABOUT SOCCER TECHNIQUE

Fisting and deflecting

Of course it's always best if you can catch the ball. It is safe and your team can begin another offensive. But sometimes the ball can't be held.

Fisting means that you hit the ball with your fist, thereby moving it as far as possible out of the danger zone.

Keep your thumb out so it doesn't get injured.

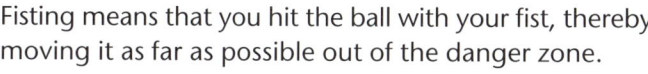

If the shot is too hard, try to deflect the ball over the goal or to the side with the flat of your hand.

 Learning Soccer

The shot angle

If you as goalie stay on the goal line, the shooter has plenty of room to score a goal. But if you run out to meet him you shorten the shot angle and the shooter has fewer opportunities to get the ball past you.

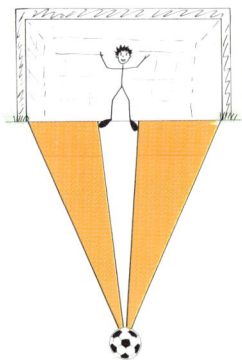

You can see this in these illustrations.

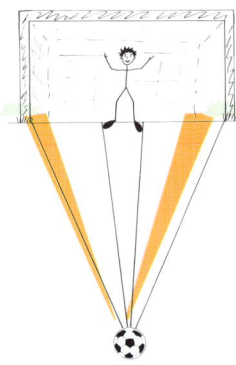

A LITTLE SOMETHING ABOUT SOCCER TECHNIQUE

Give it your all

A team depends a lot on the performance of the goalie. Often only one goal is the difference between victory, defeat or a draw. That is why the goalie has to give his or her all.

Because the goalie isn't always in the exact line of fire, it is necessary to dive for the ball. That requires courage and practice. Watch the experienced goalies and try to do what they do. But you shouldn't wear nice clothes to do this!

Puzzle

1. The front opening of each goal.
2. A violation.
3. Pass immediately preceding a goal.
4. An alliance of teams.
5. The 5-minute rest period between periods of a game.
6. Another name for goal line.

The letters in the first column will tell you what the player defending the goal is called.

DRIBBLING, FEINTS, TAKING-ON AND MOVING THE BALL

....................10 DRIBBLING, FEINTS, TAKING-ON AND MOVING THE BBALL

"The ball comes to the player. He takes it on and runs with it as fast as he can. He keeps the ball very close to his foot so it won't roll away.

Now here come the players from the opposite team. They are trying to take the ball away from him, but he doesn't give them a chance. He alternates his feet, moves forward and back, and keeps his body between the ball and the opponent.

He has completed a pass to a team-mate. He gets free again and the ball is coming back to him. He shakes off his opponents with a quick run with the ball.

He's headed for the goal, and ...scores!"

Surely you have tried to play that way many times. But it probably hasn't been as successful as it was described here. But that's alright. You need lots of soccer skill and experience for that. You are still a soccer beginner and are trying to learn.

This is what you have to learn and practice:

- *Dribbling (ball control).*
- *Feints (selling the opponent a dummy).*
- *Taking-on and moving the ball.*

On the following pages you will find more about dribbling, something about feints and about taking-on and moving the ball on.

LEARNING SOCCER

Dribbling

Dribbling is what the soccer player calls the skillful guiding of the ball with the feet without letting the opponent reach the ball or letting the ball roll away. Dribbling can be very successful because you can play around the opponent with the ball at your foot and leave him behind. You can then shoot at goal without pressure, or make a pass to a team-mate. Most of the great soccer players are good dribblers, who can skillfully shield the ball and protect it from opposing attacks.

What makes dribbling in soccer useful?

- If an opponent launches a direct assault you can play around him.
- You can run past an opponent and shake him off with the ball at your foot.
- You can lure an opponent to you and then pass the ball to a team-mate just in time. It is a way to sell the opponent a dummy.

DRIBBLING, FEINTS, TAKING-ON AND MOVING THE BALL

This is how you dribble

Learning the technique for dribbling isn't all that difficult. You drive the ball along in front of you as you run, giving it small pushes so it doesn't roll too far ahead. You use both feet and touch the ball with the inside or the outside of your foot, as well as the instep or the sole of your foot. Try not to look at the ball too much, but look at where you are going and keep an eye on your opponents and team-mates.

Keep the ball close to your foot and don't let it roll away. Initially you will use your strong foot. That's the foot you play best with. But soon you should also use your weaker foot so the opponent can't read you as easily. When you keep your body between the ball and the opponent you are able to shield the ball well. If you are on the opposing team's end of the field, run fast and take risks. But you shouldn't dribble in front of your own goal. It's too dangerous. Once you have successfully dribbled around your opponent or have left him behind, quickly finish your dribbling. Either pass the ball to a team-mate or take a shot at goal.

Only dribble when ...

- **you don't have a team-mate in a better position close by.**
- **there is plenty of space for dribbling.**
- **there is only one opponent, or the goalie, left in front of you.**

Don't overdue it with the dribbling! You might lose the ball too often and your team-mates are getting themselves free for nothing.

In Chapter 8 you already learned how to keep the ball securely at your foot.

Here are a few additional exercises.

1 Slalom

Look for obstacles you can dribble around. Those could be trees, poles, or objects. Maybe you can even have your friends stand there.

DRIBBLING, FEINTS, TAKING-ON AND MOVING THE BALL

2 Round a course

Mark out a course. On a concrete surface you can use chalk, on some other surface you can use a stick to scratch the ground, or on grass you can use a long piece of string.

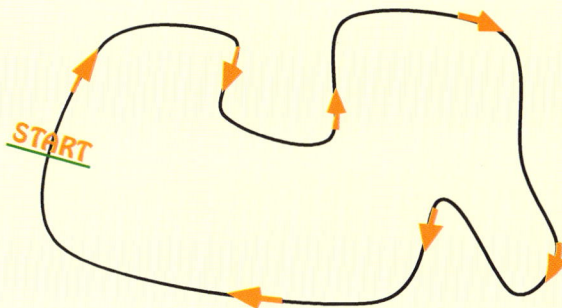

Now dribble the ball along this course. How many times can you go around without losing the ball? How long does it take you to complete one round?

3 Without looking

A soccer player shouldn't just look at the ball while dribbling. He has to watch his opponents and look for free team-mates.

Place the ball in front of your feet and look for a tree or a fence or some other object as a target. Now walk towards it with the ball at your foot and without looking at the ball.

The feint

If you want to get past an opponent with the ball at your foot you have to either be faster than him or sell him a dummy. You pretend to be running or playing in one direction and when the opponent starts to move in the same direction you go past him on the opposite side. That is the idea and purpose of the feint. Later when you have more experience you can even look in the "wrong" direction, or call to the "wrong" teammate.

The more skillful you are the easier it will be to outplay your opponent.

You have to conceal your intentions, feint round the opponent, and use all sorts of tricks to be successful.

Billy is practicing glancing feints

Why feints are so important

 You can use a feint to get past an opponent, to get closer to the goal and have a clear shot at the goal.

 You leave your opponent standing, and together with your teammates, achieve a superior number. In that particular situation your team would have one player more and you could play to that unguarded player. This would increase your chances of scoring a goal.

 You are stealing your opponent's self-confidence because he is falling for your tricks and body feints and can't get at the ball. This angers him and makes him weaker. You are on the road to victory. It is said that whoever wins the majority of one-on-one fights in soccer usually wins the game.

 With tricks and feints you can avoid one-on-one situations, keep from getting injured, and can continue your action after you have dribbled around.

The step feint

With your right foot bring the ball toward your opponent. Then just in time make a wide lunge to the left with your left foot. You opponent will follow that move (also called standing on the wrong foot), and then you suddenly pass him on the right with the ball at your foot.

Act quickly when the opponent makes that wrong move and run past him. If you are approaching from the right, play the ball on the right outside and immediately put some distance between yourself and the opponent.

This is how you can learn feints:

 Practice the sequence of the feint by yourself without an opponent and try to memorize the movements.

 Find a tree, a pole, or a plastic cone and imagine it is your opponent. Practice the sequence like that. This opponent won't harm you and won't take the ball away from you. But you will learn the feint sequence, how fast you need to be, when to start the feint, and which direction you have to run.

 Now practice with a human opponent. Surely your mother, father, grandfather, or friend would have fun practicing with you. They can react to your feint without taking the ball away from you.

 Now it gets serious! Find a real opponent who will seriously try to take the ball away from you. Plan how you will trick him and don't tell him. Try it and see if your plan succeeds.

Receiving and moving the ball on

Nowadays soccer has become very fast. The player hardly has time to stop the approaching ball and then figure out how to proceed. Everything has to happen quickly and seamlessly. The ball is taken on and immediately moved along into a new direction or passed. That way the opponent has fewer chances to take the ball away from you.

Taking-on and moving a ball is what makes good team work happen within the team and secures possession of the ball.

How do you receive the ball?

 With any part of both feet:

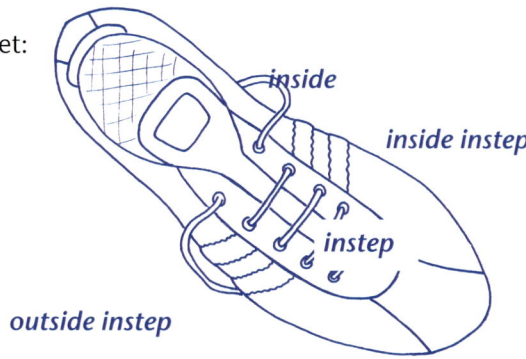

inside
inside instep
instep
outside instep

 With other parts of the body:
- head
- chest
- thighs

DRIBBLING, FEINTS, TAKING-ON AND MOVING THE BALL

What are the guidelines for receiving and moving the ball on?

How a ball is received and moved on is determined by the velocity with which the ball arrives, and whether it is a low, medium high or a high ball. The distance of the ball is also a deciding factor. When choosing a technique the player has to consider the amount of time and space available to control the ball.

Receiving and moving on low balls

For beginners the safest and easiest way to learn ball control for receiving and moving the ball is with the inside of the foot. This technique is applied most often in the early stages of learning soccer, because the ball is passed mostly low and rolling.

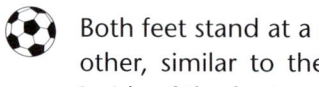

What you need to pay attention to:

- Both feet stand at a right angle to each other, similar to the side kick with the inside of the foot.

- The inside of the receiving foot slightly approaches the ball and receives it giving just a little. This is important so that the ball lands softly on your foot. If you don't do it like this the ball will bounce away and become easy prey for your opponent.

- Lift the toe of your playing leg just a little. Now the ball won't be able to roll over your foot or bounce up.

- Immediately after receiving the ball you need to move it in another direction (that's why we call it taking-on and moving it on). This way you can disengage yourself from the opposing attack.

- Try to combine receiving the ball with a feint as often as possible. When you receive or move the ball on with the inside of the foot, you can swing your leg as though you were going to kick the approaching ball. Then the opponent won't know whether you are really going to take on the ball or if you are going to pass it to a team-mate.

Take another look at the technique for the side kick with the inside of the foot!

DRIBBLING, FEINTS, TAKING-ON AND MOVING THE BALL

If you've already developed a better feel for the ball you can also take on and move on low balls with the outside of the foot.

That's when you receive the incoming ball with the outside of your strong foot next to the supporting leg, and immediately move it on into another direction. You will need to turn the foot of the playing leg to the inside and point the toe upwards.

Here you can also trick the opponent before you receive the ball. Take a step to the left and with the outside of your other foot take the ball along to the right. This move is executed the same way as the step feint on Page 96.

This is how you can practice:

 Play against a wall. Receive the returning ball with the inside or the outside of the foot.

 Have someone play the ball to you. Receive it and run with it for a short distance, then play it back again

Taking-on and moving
high, bouncing, and fast approaching balls on

You can receive high balls with your foot, or your thigh, your torso, or even with your head.

receiving with the chest

receiving with the foot

receiving with the thigh

But this technique is pretty difficult and probably more suited for advanced players. That's why we won't give a detailed description here.

What's important to you as a beginner:

Try to gain control of bouncing and fast approaching balls as quickly as possible and get them back on the ground. Then it will be easier for you, and the team will work better together.

DRIBBLING, FEINTS, TAKING-ON AND MOVING THE BALL

 Try this at home:

Throw the ball high against a wall. When the ball returns let it fall on your thigh, then pull your thigh back and let the ball land softly as you would when using the inside of your foot. The ball will lie in front of your feet ready to be played.

 It is more difficult to receive the ball with your instep or your chest, or with your head. After gaining quick control you can continue playing it on the ground with your feet.

LEARNING SOCCER

Playing soccer with friends is the best!

You'll have lots of fun practicing together. Have some competitions and form teams. Good soccer buddies help each other and point out each other's mistakes during practice.

11 Let's Play!

You don't necessarily need two teams of 11 players, two goals, and a referee to play soccer with your friends at school or in the yard. Soccer is also really fun on smaller fields with fewer players. Besides, when you play with fewer people you have more opportunity to practice your technique and improve your soccer skills. That's exactly what our playing suggestions on the next few pages are for.

No matter how many players you have, if you are playing on a small field with only one goal, – have a great time playing soccer!

Find a suitable place for playing and set up goals. Be careful that there aren't any windows or flower beds close by that could be damaged by loose balls. Avoid freshly painted surfaces and don't play near heavily traveled roads. Ready? Let's start!

Shooting and goal

The most important thing is that you get the ball to go where it's supposed to go as accurately as possible and with the right amount of power. That would be the goal, a team-mate, or sometimes the safety of a throw-in.

Of course that doesn't happen automatically. You need to develop a feel for the ball, the direction, the distance, and for your shooting power. On the next few pages you will find exercises for shooting at goal and variations on playing that you can practice by yourself or with your friends. The type of kick doesn't really matter at this point. Execute the goal shot any way you like. You'll soon learn which type of kick is best in a particular situation. Do you want to change the rules of play? No problem! Play your own variation. Have a great time!

The most important thing is that you get the ball to go where it's supposed to go as accurately as possible and with the right amount of power.

Practice shots on target and at goals of different sizes and from varying distances, so you can figure out which kick to use and how much power to put behind it.

Shooting at goal with two players

Set up two goals approximately 50 yards apart. Each goal should be about 15 feet wide. Now try to score goals against each other. The type of kick used is up to you.

LET'S PLAY

Target shooting

Set up a goal about 4 feet wide, take five steps back and shoot at the goal with the inside of the foot.

Every time you score, take an additional five steps back, thereby increasing the degree of difficulty. How far away can you get and how long can you still score with the inside of the foot? Try to gange how much power you need to apply. Who will be able to score from the greatest distance with the inside of the foot?

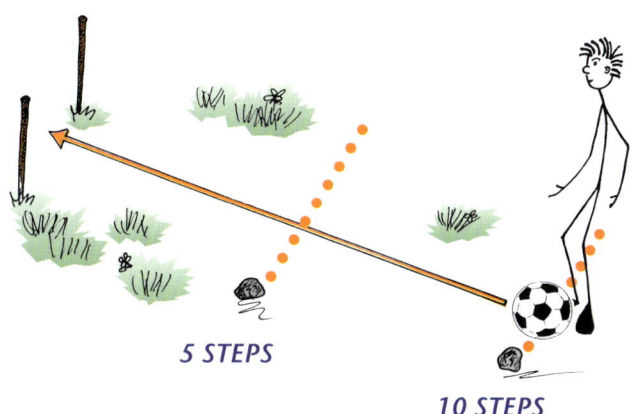

5 STEPS

10 STEPS

Distance shooting

Who can kick the ball farthest? You can measure where the ball lands or where it stops once it's finished rolling.

Learning Soccer

Power shot (ball doesn't bounce)

Try to kick a power shot into a regular size goal with the full instep or the inside of the foot from a distance of about 20 yards. Choose the kick yourself and decide which one is more accurate. It only counts as a goal if the ball crosses the goal line in flight.

Kicking deep

To develop shooting power and shooting technique you can play kicking the ball deep down the pitch with a friend. On a large playing field or another large area you will need to mark a neutral zone of approximately 30 yards in the center of the field.

Each player has an equal sized large field behind him to defend. The first player (you can draw lots) kicks the resting ball as far as he can into the opposing half. The opposing player shoots the ball from where it landed, in turn trying to push it back as far as he can.

Whoevers ball crosses the opponent's rear defense line (base line) first is the winner.

Player 1	Neutral zone	Player 2

LET'S PLAY

Shoot out

For this game you will need a ball, a goal, and at least six players. Everyone except for the shooter stands in the goal. The shooter places the ball about 15 yards from the goal and tries to score. Whoever lets the ball through is out. If the ball is held the shooter goes in the goal and the player on the far right takes his turn as shooter. Whoever is left in the end is the winner.

Eleven … Twelve

There is one goal and any given number of players. The first player calls out: "Eleven!", and all the other players follow on from him. The last one will be goalie. Each field player has 11 points and the goalie has twelve points.

Now the field players play the ball to each other, whereby the ball has to be passed as soon as contact has been made. Anyone who thinks he has a chance tries a shot on goal. If he scores, the goalie gets a one-point deduction. If he misses the shooter gets a one-point deduction and becomes goalie. If you like you can also give away points for super goals like headers or bicycle kicks.

LEARNING SOCCER

8 Soccer tennis

Play lots of soccer tennis! Instead of a racket you use your foot or your head to play the ball over a net or a piece of string about 3 feet off the ground. Try to keep the ball in play as long as possible.

This game is good for developing a feel for the ball, and almost all types of kicks are used.

Elite

Elite means finding out who's the best. It is the perfect game for practicing shooting technique and shooting strength.

Draw a 15 to 22 foot wide goal on a wall in chalk. Any given number of players line up about 7 yards from the goal. The first player kicks the ball against the wall into the goal. The next player has to receive the ball as it bounces back and immediately kick it at the goal. Whoever misses the ball or the goal is out.

Try to shoot in a way that makes it difficult for the next player to take a shot.

 Learning Soccer

 **Team play**

It's best if you can form two teams to play against each other. Since the number of friends turning up to play usually varies, you can try out different game variations.

Here are some ideas:

With *two* players
Each player sets up a goal. While playing against each other try to score against the other player while defending your own goal.

With *three* players
One goal is being defended by one goalie. The other players play against that goal. Whoever scores becomes the goalie.

LET'S PLAY

With *four* players
Two teams with two players in each. They play against each other using two small goals.

With *five* players
One goal is defended by one goalie. Each team has two players playing against that goal.

With *six* players
Each team has three players playing against each other using two goals. The ball cannot be stopped by hand. The player farthest back is goalie.

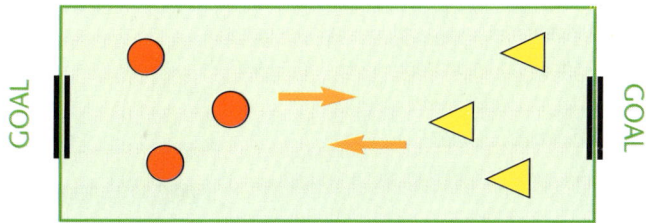

With *seven* players
Two teams of three players play against one goal being defended by one goalie.

How could you play with eight players?

_____

_____

Learning Soccer

A few tips!

- *You set up the rules of play yourselves. Decide how to play and what would be the most fun.*

- *Distances don't have to be measured exactly. One big step or two small steps are approximately one yard.*

- *If you want to form teams, choose two game captains, who alternately choose their sides.*

Who starts to choose?

"Coffee beans" are steps you take putting one foot right in front of the other heel to toe. Both players walk toward each other.

Whoever steps on the other's foot first gets to choose first.

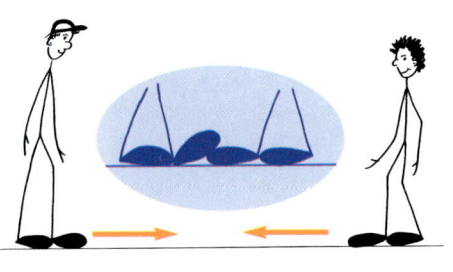

"Eenie- Meenie- Minie- Moe, catch a tiger by the toe. If he hollers let him go. Eenie-Meenie-Minie-Moe!"

..........12 Playing for a Soccer Club

The day will come when you think that playing soccer on the playground or in the backyard just isn't enough anymore. That's when it's time to join a league. There you can play on a team, be involved in the game organization, and play in real competitions.

How do you join a league?

 Ask your parents for permission. If they agree then you can start looking for a league in your area.

 Most sports organizations have a bulletin board where phone numbers and training schedules are posted.

LEARNING SOCCER

- Find out when tryouts are scheduled. There you can watch how everything works. You meet the coaches and the other kids and see how they train. Of course everything is new and strange. But that's totally normal.

- Usually you are asked how old you are and which age group you should be placed in. That's how placement on a team is done in a league. It depends on the year you were born, not what school grade you are in.

The age groups

Age	Team Classification
5-6 years	U6
7-8 years	U8
9-10 years	U10
11-12 years	U12
13-14 years	U14
15-16 years	U16
17-18 years	U18

- Girls and boys usually play together until age 12. Starting with U14, girls and boys play separately.

- Now you are being tried out for a league of your choice. Your parents or grandparents should accompany you. Bring your gym clothes, and tennis shoes or soccer boots.

- If you like it and the coach says that you are suited for playing soccer, you should sign up. You'll become a member of the club and may even get a membership card.

My first soccer club

Club name: _____

Entry date: _____

My coaches: _____

My team:
(names, signatures)

Our colors: _____

Our logo:

Keep track of the scores here:

Opponents	Score

What does a club and team member have to do?

- Pay a membership fee.
- Take good care of the club playing strip.
- Buy soccer boots.
- Wear shin guards.

What does the club have to do?

- Insure the players against sport related accidents and injuries.
- Organize the training and game programs.
- Issue a membership card to the player.
- Provide the playing strip and may be even launder them.
- Organize transportation to and from games.
- The club has coaches and organizers.

What if I want to leave the club or switch to another club?

If you want to leave the club or switch over to another club you need to cancel your membership, possibly in writing. Sometimes there are restrictions on being able to change clubs.

Do I always have to go to practice?

- Punctuality and regularity are important in sports. Otherwise you won't learn anything.
- If you can't make practice, excuse yourself with the coach or the organizer.
- Schoolwork always comes before practice.

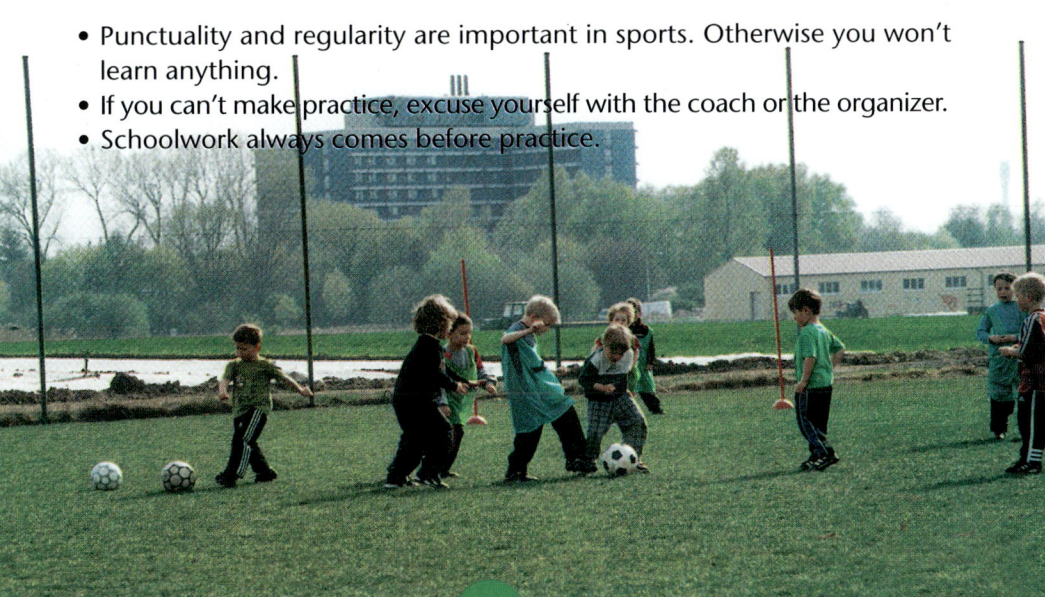

 Learning Soccer

How can I continue to advance as a soccer player?

You already read the interview with Ulf Kirsten and learned how he went from playing as a child to becoming a top player in the German National League (Bundesliga). If you too want to achieve more, the road ahead may look something like this:

- Once you get to level U12 or U14 you may want to switch to a more high-level club.
- If you are good you may make it onto a select team in elementary school.
- Middle schools and high schools generally have select teams. At the high school level you can also try out for Junior Varsity and Varsity. Often coaches from private high schools will recruit players from other schools for their varsity teams.
- Soccer at the college level offers three main divisions of which level one is the best.
- On a national level there is a youth developmental program starting at the U14 level.
- The U16 level marks eligibility for the Boys National Team.
- Eligibility for the Men's National team begins at level U17 and goes to the over 23 level.
- The men's professional soccer league is the MLS (Major League Soccer), and the women's professional soccer league is the WUSA.

.... 13 LITTLE SOCCER ENCYCLOPEDIA

Coach	Another word for trainer.
Condition	A player's physical condition, to be fit enough to play a whole game.
Covering	Positional play to keep the opponent from getting possession of the ball.
Cross	Passing the ball parallel to the goal lines.
Dive	Falling down without an opposing foul to deceive the referee and prompt a free kick or a penalty kick.
Dribbling	Playing around the opponent with the ball at your foot.
Draw	Both teams have scored the same number of goals.
English week	Game rhythm decided on points modeled after the English league.
Extra time	Extended playing time used in finals to determine a winner.
Fan	Follower of a team.
Feel for the ball	The players feel for the ball and its movement.
Feint	Deceiving the opponent/selling a dummy.
Foul	Illegal action against the opponent, punishable by a free kick.
Free kick	Continuation of the game after a foul.
Goal	Structure at which the ball is being aimed, also countable result of a game.
Halftime	Time measure for one half of a game.
Hat trick	Three goals scored during one half by one player.
Hooligan	Rioters have no business at soccer games.
Indirect free kick	The ball must be touched by another player on the way into the goal.

 Learning Soccer

International match...	International competition between two teams from different nations.
Juggling	Keeping the ball in the air without touching the ground.
National team	A country's select team.
Offensive	A team's continued efforts to attack.
One-on-one	Two players competing for the possession of the ball.
Out	The ball went over one of the sidelines. Throw-in.
Pass	Playing the ball to a team-mate.
Penalty shoot-out ..	Determining a winner at the end of a final game after a draw or extra time.
Pro	Someone who earns his money playing soccer.
Red card	The highest penalty against a player. Player is sent off the field for the rest of the game.
Side or spin	The ball has an arched trajectory with a spin.
Substitution	One player leaves the field, another one comes on.
Tackling	Literally taking the ball away from the opponent or separating the opponent from the ball.
Tactic	Plan or strategy to defeat the opponent.
Technique	The type of ball control and ball treatment.
Yellow card	Penalty against a player violating the rules of play.
Wall	The players form a defensive block in front of their goal to fend off an opposing free kick.

Here you can write down some more words and expressions you want to remember.

............14 SOLUTIONS AND ANSWERS

Pg. 17   There are 14 hidden leather balls.

Pg. 18   Eyes, mouth, hatband, folds on hat, ball is turned, pant pocket, pant waist, left sleeve at wrist, left shoelace, right sock

Pg. 32   Number 3 scores the goal.
Numbers 3 and 5 are the same.

Pg. 33   Foods a soccer player should not eat.

Pg. 41   It's a square ball.
No. 3 is the missing piece.

Pg. 48   1 Stealing the ball from the opponent is legal.
2 Kicking at a player's legs or tripping him is illegal.

Pg. 49   3 Elbowing the opponent in the face is illegal.
4 Holding on to the opponents clothing or body is illegal.
5 The leg is too high (dangerous play). That's illegal.
6 Jostling and pressing are legal.

Pg. 50   The girl is playing the ball with her arm. That's called "handball".
   1 Free kick
   2 warning (yellow card) or send-off (red card)
   3 Continue play – advantage

Pg. 65   The ball travels downward.

Pg. 68   1 The toe of the supporting leg is not pointing in the direction of play.
2 The torso is not bent over the ball, but leans back too far.
3 The ankle of the playing leg is not rigid and the foot is angled downward.

Pg. 73   1 The torso is leaning back too far.
2 The player is kicking the ball with her toe instead of her instep.
3 The supporting leg is too far away from the ball.

Pg. 79   1 When the ball approaches the body becomes taut like a bow. Don't lean forward!
2 The player is closing his eyes during a header.
3 The ball must be butted with the forehead and not the top of the head.

Pg. 88

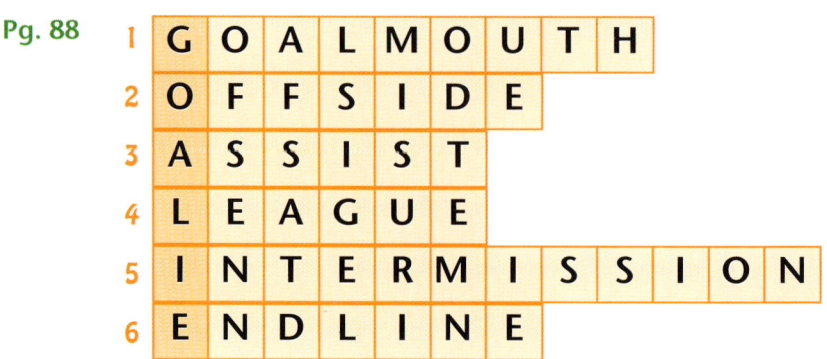

Pg. 113   If you have eight players, you can form two teams of four. Play against each other using two goals. Decide amongst yourselves if one player should be a fulltime goalie.

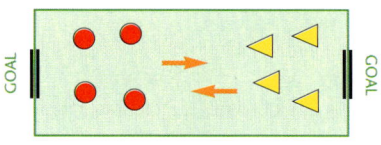

15 Let's Talk

Dear soccer parents,

Do you remember the first time your little son or daughter chased after a ball and wanted to play soccer? You'll probably say that happened as soon as he or she could walk.

What is the fascination with soccer that has so many people around the world, – young, old, men, women, and children – playing the game? And many more regularly go to a stadium, or to the local team's soccer field, or sit spellbound in front of the television. It is probably the combination of team play and individual star players, the subtle dribbling, the skillful lifts, the beautiful goals and the clever tactics.

Your child is also interested in this exceedingly popular sport and may have already decided to join a team. It is good that you are supporting this wish.

Soccer distinguishes itself through the diversity of its movements. It is demanding regarding technique, stamina, and skill, promotes concentration and quick decision making. Your child is part of a social group and is exposed to the particularities of team play, one-on-one play, as well as the importance of the individual player. He will learn to assert himself, and to cope with success and failure during games. Personal responsibility also must be learned.

Gradually the players will take responsibility for the care of their soccer boots and the completeness of their equipment, as well as being punctual,

Learning Soccer

and regularly attending practices and competitions. Please support your child in learning to play soccer, practicing, and training.

With our little players the delight in the game, the movements, and the shooting of goals are initially totally predominant. While this also requires some basic technical skills, those should not present the overall focus at this time. The kids should play, have fun and at the same time develop their skills.

That is also the purpose of this book. Aside from explaining necessary technical skills and soccer rules, soccer kids find out lots of general information about the game of soccer. They have the opportunity to become actively involved with their favorite sport. Preschoolers and readers who are beginners will still require their parents' help with reading and taking notes.

Help, but discreetly, please!

Be careful not to expect too much from your child. What matters most is enjoying the sport and the game. Excessive ambition can be damaging. Don't make comparisons between your child and other children of the same age. Biological development can still vary greatly at this age. Just focus on your own child and praise his or her progress. Your child will thank you!

Support from soccer parents

Particularly in soccer, support from soccer parents is in great demand. Or are you not familiar with the stack of dirty playing strip, the kids playing noisily outside your home, or the desperate wish for a real pair of soccer boots or a soccer ball? But as soon as your child has joined a league, the family weekends revolve around the soccer schedule. If there is a game on Saturday or Sunday, breakfast is dictated by the alarm clock, the parents are chauffeurs for part of the team, and the rest of the family wants to come along to cheer on the team. The Sunday roast has to wait, and until the final whistle-blow any outings or visits to grandparents can only be scheduled for no-game days.

But what's better than seeing your little mud-covered, sweating soccer player irrepressibly happy about his first goal. Or the reassurance and closeness parents and child share when some consoling becomes necessary after a defeat or a substitution. Be glad your child is getting some regular exercise. It doesn't matter if your little player will some day be a soccer star, or even if he is "only" enjoying the game and the camaraderie.

One more thing:
A parent shouting at the players during a game only confuses the children. The children need to make their own decisions, and it is the coach's job to take care of any technical details and substitutions.

Dad, – our coach

The first coaches, not only at home but also on the playground, are often dads or older brothers. Often they are the coaches or assistant coaches for the team who teach the little ones the soccer ABC's. One remembers one's own training and tries to make a team out of that wild bunch.

This book provides many suggestions to all those motivated lay-coaches for the continued training of their charges.

LET'S TALK

Dear soccer coach,

Who amongst us isn't familiar with the sight of the little beginners in soccer chasing after the ball! Without any order but with much impetuousness they are fixated on the ball. They drive the ball until at some point it finally lands in the goal. Most often it is the fastest one amongst them who rushes off and without delay deposits the ball in the goal. It is a wonderful image and reminder of the past from the ever recurring beginnings of soccer, playing on fields and on playgrounds.

Years ago, in the days of street soccer, there were no such phenomena. The concept of "everyone after the ball" was suppressed due to the maturity of the older and more experienced players on the heterogeneously composed street team. They guided the younger and less experienced players, placed them in positions appropriate to their skill level, and whoever just didn't get it was criticized, or in the worst case scenario, eliminated or not chosen again.

In today's league training, where these kinds of heterogeneous teams don't exist anymore, all children are approximately the same age and therefore all beginners or 'newbies' together.

There are leagues for children as young as five or six years old and many of the junior leagues have teams for specific age groups. And now it's up to the trainer, usually a father or older sibling, to make an orderly, cohesive team out of a swarm of bees fixated on the ball.

How do I teach these lively little guys to play?

The little guys want to play and experience success. But that requires lots of contact with the ball and shots at goal.

In a game of 11 on 11 on a huge field, only the fast and the strong excel. The smaller and more delicate ones make very little contact with the ball,

and the goalies and defensive players of the dominant team just stand around at the back and hardly touch the ball. That will make it hard for them to get into a game that was so fascinating on television.

That is why we recommend using the game ideas we introduced in the book:

Play on a smaller field with smaller teams.

- The kids want to have fun playing soccer; to be able to give free reign to their inborn play instinct, just like they used to do in street soccer. Kids got together to kick the ball around, just for the sheer fun of playing on the street.

- Children have a natural desire to move with many, sometimes sweeping, quick, occasionally quite uncoordinated movements. These genetically predisposed patterns should not be disrupted.

- Children play soccer to physically compete with other children. They want to prove themselves, determine who's strongest, fastest, most skillful, the best technician, goal scorer and goalie.

- Children enjoy competitions against others. They always want to have the most accurately measured results in their competition with each other. It's all about victory and defeat, and only rarely are they content with a draw.

- Children want to have fun and enjoy themselves playing soccer. It should happen in a relaxed atmosphere. No stress, no pressure, but a wonderful experience of succeeding as a group, but also experiencing the sorrow of defeat. Experiencing success and processing failure helps children grow.

- Children need free play. No tactical constraints ("You play at the very back, and make sure you stay there!"), no collective commands ("We are going to force an offside!") They should be able to construct their own game, creatively, according to their skill level and ability.

- Children should be allowed to develop the concept of playing the big game on their own. They learn by trial and error, not by drilling and loud instructions from the sidelines. They learn by way of experimentation, repetition, emulation, action, comparison, condemnation and memorization.

In short: They learn the game by playing it!

What makes a good children's coach

None of these children are alike. There are the diligent ones and the less diligent ones, the talented ones and the not so talented ones, the precocious ones and the late bloomers.

Each of these children is a unique individual with individual qualifications and a unique developed background, with hopes and desires, with existential orientations and needs. All of them deserve our attention, our care and our love.

The better a soccer coach can relate to his soccer kids, the more he can sympathize, the more he can approach and inspire them, the more effective he will be. He must spur them on and listen to them; he must be able to put himself in their position, to praise and comfort them, – in short, he must have a heart for children. Occasionally he must be able to cool down or reprimand a hothead, but always do so with respect for their own little personality.

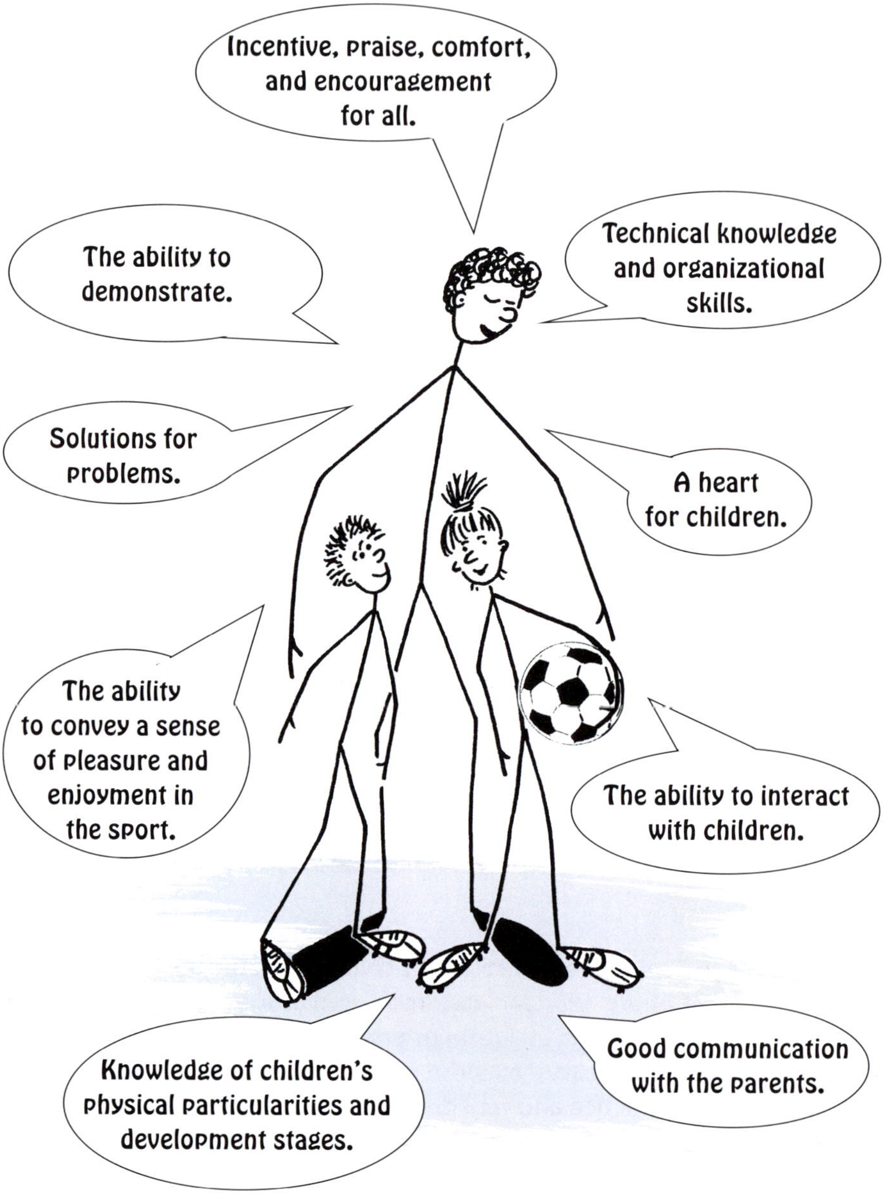

LET'S TALK

The value of this little book

The value of this little book depends entirely on how it is integrated into soccer education. It is written specifically for children in the beginning stages of training or children practicing at home. But it is also recommended for parents who want to accompany their child on this path.

Most of the instructional guides and books about soccer give insufficient consideration to the actual participants, the players themselves, although they are the most important part of the teaching – and learning process. A soccer player, no matter how young and totally inexperienced he may be, is always subject to his or her own development, and never just an object for us to manipulate. So offer them sufficient consideration and opportunity for their own growth. Promote and utilize their independence. Take the path from instructing to inspiring. Beginner soccer players don't have to or must, but they can and they may.

This book focuses on the children's needs and is intended to help them engage in soccer off the playing field as well as on. The illustrations and descriptions of the most important techniques in this book give the child quite a complete basis of information for practicing. He or she will be able to follow more easily your instructions and demonstrations. The up-and-coming soccer players can re-read what they learned at their leisure, while getting suggestions for practice at home and with other children. This helps promote independent action and speeds up the learning process.

An environment is created in which the children are encouraged to think about their practicing and learning, their movements and actions, and lastly to examine and to evaluate their performance, all in a step by step process. You will be a partner to the coach. We want children to enjoy coming to soccer practice and go home with a sense of success. And that of course makes the practice sessions more fun for the coach as well.

LEARNING SOCCER

In closing we would like to offer some suggestions on how to apply this book in your work as a soccer coach:

- Tell the children that this book is their personal companion while learning to play soccer. Give them a copy of the team logo and take a group photo to paste in the book. This promotes their bonding with you and the club.

- Help the children to use the book properly. In the beginning, read sections together and explain how the photos and illustrations should be viewed and understood. By doing so you provide the children with important orientation guides for understanding and independent practice.

- Have them actually do the suggested practice activities. You demonstrate, explain, and practice new techniques or actions during practice sessions. Then there's the homework: "Review this technique at home. Anyone who wants to can explain and demonstrate it to the rest of us next practice session."

- We tried to write the book in language that is appropriate to children of all ages, and included graphic explanations whenever possible. By using the same or similar phrasing you can ensure a common basis for communication within the practice group, and cut down on explanations and corrections during practice sessions. This will free up more time for actual practicing.

We welcome any critical commentaries or additions.

We wish you and your little protégées lots of fun and enjoyment, and of course many soccer successes.

Photo and illustration credits

Cover Design: Birgit Engelen, Stolberg
Illustrations: Katrin Barth
Cover Photo: Sportpressefoto Bongarts Hamburg
Photos (inside): Bayer 04 Leverkusen, Gerd Schumacher,
Kerstin Dischereit, Birgit Küspert, TV Rheinbeck
Siegfried Zebisch

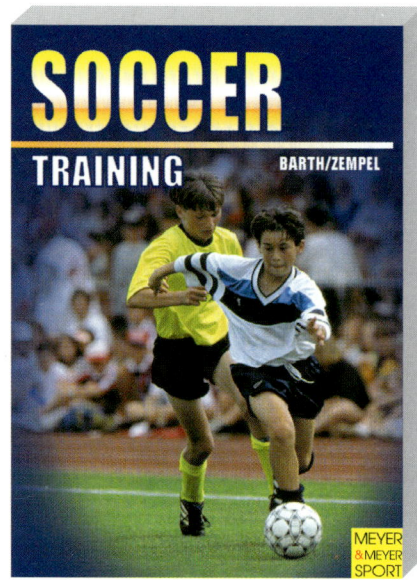

Barth/Zempel
Training ... Soccer

Your child wants to get serious about soccer training – but what's the best approach? This book endeavors to answer that question in a manner to which children can readily respond. A training companion and workbook in one, it takes up where "Learning Soccer" leaves off. Readers additionally receive excellent, challenging and age-appropriate information covering a full range of topics including physical condition, mental preparation, etc.

152 pages
Full-colour print, some photos
numerous drawings
Paperback, 5 $^{3}/_{4}$" x 8 $^{1}/_{4}$"
ISBN 1-84126-131-9
£ 9.95 UK/$ 14.95 US
$ 20.95 CDN/€ 14.90

MEYER & MEYER Sport | Von-Coels-Straße 390 | D-52080 Aachen | Fax +49 (0)2 41- 9 58 10-10